S0-CFS-988

JUL 2 2 2008

When I Was Five

by Arthur Howard

Voyager Books • Harcourt, Inc.

Orlando   Austin   New York   San Diego   Toronto   London

Ypsilanti District Library
5577 Whittaker Road
Ypsilanti, MI 48197

Copyright © 1996 by Arthur Howard

All rights reserved. No part of this publication may be reproduced
or transmitted in any form or by any means, electronic or mechanical,
including photocopy, recording, or any information storage and
retrieval system, without permission in writing from the publisher.

Requests for permission to make copies of any part of the work
should be mailed to the following address: Permissions Department,
Harcourt, Inc., 6277 Sea Harbor Drive, Orlando, Florida, 32887-6777.

www.HarcourtBooks.com

First Voyager Books edition 1999
Voyager Books is a registered trademark of Harcourt, Inc.

The Library of Congress has cataloged the hardcover edition as follows:
Howard, Arthur.
When I was five/Arthur Howard.—1st ed.
p.   cm.
Summary: A six-year-old boy describes the things he liked when
he was five and compares them to the things he likes now.
ISBN 0-15-200261-8
ISBN 0-15-202099-3 pb
[1. Growth—Fiction. 2. Identity—Fiction. 3. Friendship—Fiction.] I. Title.
PZ7.H8324Wh   1996
[E]—dc20   94-43987

K M O P N L

Printed in Singapore

The illustrations in this book were done in watercolor, gouache,
and black pencil on 90-lb. drawing paper.
The text type was hand-lettered by Arthur Howard.
Color separations by Bright Arts, Ltd., Singapore
Printed and bound by Tien Wah Press, Singapore
Production supervision by Stanley Redfern and Jane Van Gelder
Designed by Arthur Howard and Camilla Filancia

for Beverly

When I was five

or a cowboy

or both.

When I
was five
this was
my favorite
kind of
car,

this was
my favorite
kind of dinosaur,

and this was my
best friend, Mark.

Mark had a dog named Peggy,

a brother who used bad words,

and bunk beds—
my favorite
kind of bed
when I was five.

Now I'm six

BABE RUTH

Cal RIPKEN Jr

and I want to be a

major-league baseball player

or a deep-sea diver.

this is my favorite kind of car,

this is my favorite
kind of dinosaur,

this is my second-best hiding place
(my favorite one is a secret),

and this is my best friend, Mark.

Some things never change.